"I understand completely," said X22.

Then he tucked his saucer into his belt for safekeeping.

"Let's go," he said, beaming.

And the two elephant friends flew back to earth
and Arthur's saucer.

The End

"How can I ever thank you?" said X22.

"No need to," said Arthur. "But I am getting awfully hungry."

"Have some stardust," said X22.

"Stardust isn't my cup of tea," said Arthur. "And anyway I can't eat unless I eat out of my saucer with my name on it and my saucer's back home."

until he was full and dazzling!

Then he ate,

and ate,

and ate.

And the more he ate the more he glowed. And he ate and glowed and ate and glowed —

X22 was practically out like a light, but he managed to stagger over to his saucer. He picked it up and caught some stardust.

"Everybody thinks I'm a nasty, hard-hearted old elephant,
but I'm really a sentimental old fool. Take your saucer, X22!"
"Since you're such a softie," said Arthur, "I suppose you're
not going to take my telescope."
"That's what you think," said Honest Tom, drying his tears.
"A bargain's a bargain!"

"Wait —" said Arthur.

"Take my telescope for X22's saucer!"

"You mean you'd be willing to swap your expensive telescope
for X22's cheap but old saucer?" asked Honest Tom.

"Yes," said Arthur.

Honest Tom burst into tears.

"That's real friendship," he cried. "True friendship."

He took out his handkerchief and blew his trunk.

"That still doesn't prove anything," said Tom. "It could be
a forgery. Do you have proper identification with you? Driver's
license, birth certificate, credit cards, marriage license, social
security number, money?"

"No," said X22. "I don't even have a wallet."

"Well, then, I'm sorry," said Honest Tom. "Business is
business."

"Can I help you elephants?" asked Honest Tom himself.

"I want my saucer!" said X22.

"What do you mean, *your* saucer?" asked Honest Tom. "Does it have your name on it?"

"As a matter of fact, it does," said X22.

And there sat Honest Tom.

Arthur and X22 flew to the correct star.

About X22's saucer — Honest Tom, the antique flying saucer
collector, has just added it to his collection. You'll find his
place of business on the star to my left."

"Thank you very much," said Arthur.

"Always glad to help elephants in distress,"
said the Elephant in the Moon.

Arthur and X22 flew up to see the Elephant in the Moon.

"The king sent us," said Arthur.

"I know," said the Elephant in the Moon.

"I know all, see all, and tell all.

Ask me no questions, I'll tell you no lies.

But the Man in the Moon has very big eyes."

"I think he's trying to tell us something," said Arthur.

"I hope so," sighed X22.

"In plain talk," said the king, "ask the Elephant in the Moon.

Tell him I sent you."

"One, two,
What to do?
Three, four,
What a bore.
Five, six,
You're in a fix.
Seven, eight,
Don't hesitate.
Nine, ten,
Mice or men?

"Speaking of dishes, Your Majesty," said Arthur,
"we're looking for a saucer with my friend's name on it."
"What's your friend's name?" asked the king.
"X22," said Arthur.
"That's not a name, that's a number," said the king.

The king was in his countinghouse counting all his money.
He peered over stacks of gold pieces at Arthur and X22.
"Now isn't this a tasty dish to set before the king?"
he asked.

"Tell it to the king," said a Martian who seemed to be the leader.

"We'd be glad to," said Arthur, shaking slightly.

X22 grew dimmer and dimmer.

The next moment they were surrounded by an army of
Martians.
"I come from haunts of Venus and Mars," said X22.
"And I'm his friend," said Arthur.

Suddenly a saucer flew into view! But the name on it
was Herman.
X22 was growing dimmer and dimmer.
"If I don't find my saucer soon, I'll black out," he sighed.

They passed flying cups and flying plates and flying
knives and flying forks and even a flying soup tureen —
but no flying saucer.

"I'll help you look in outer space if you'll carry me
on your back," said Arthur. "You see, I can't fly."
"You can't fly?" asked X22. "I thought *all* elephants could
fly. Well, I guess it takes all kinds. Hop on."
"Shall I begin the countdown?" asked Arthur.
"That won't be necessary," said X22.

ZOOM!

Higher and higher they flew.
"So this is outer space," said Arthur.

"Haven't seen any flying saucers," said Diamond Jim
Crocodile. "But I did see a couple of Martians.
Ate 'em. Real tasty, too."

"Flying saucers? What are you two, a couple of
crackpot elephants?" roared Lex Lion.

"Have an apple," said Sebastian Serpent. "Keeps the
doctor away."

"Please don't mention food," said X22, getting dimmer
by the minute.

"Excuse me, Mrs. Ape," said Arthur. "Have you by any chance seen a flying saucer with my friend's name on it?" Mrs. Ape thought and thought. She thought for so long that the two elephants were afraid she had gone into a trance. Finally she said, "Don't believe so."

"Flying saucer with your friend's John Hancock on it? Nope," said R. R. Rhino.

"My name is X22 and I come from haunts of
Venus and Mars looking for my flying saucer.
It flew away."
A flying saucer, thought Arthur.
"It has my name on it," said X22. "I can't
eat without my saucer, and if I don't eat
I won't glow, and if I don't glow
I'll be in the dark, and I'm afraid of the dark."
He's his own night light, thought Arthur.
But he's getting dim.
"I haven't seen your saucer," said Arthur,
"but let's ask around. There are quite a few
crackpots who might know."
"I don't mind cracked pots," said X22.
"I do mind cracked saucers."

The Unidentified Flying Elephant flew closer and closer
and closer until he and Arthur were seeing eye to eye,
with only Arthur's telescope between.

"You're awfully small," said the Unidentified Flying Elephant.

"I'm not really," said Arthur. "You're looking at me through
the wrong end of my telescope."

"Sorry," said the Unidentified Flying Elephant.

Arthur was looking for unidentified flying objects
when he saw the Unidentified Flying Elephant.

For Middy

First Printing

Library of Congress Catalog Card Number: 68-29763
Manufactured in the United States of America
Printed by Affiliated Lithographers, Inc., New York
Bound by Edition Book Bindery, New Jersey

Whitney Darrow, Jr's
UNIDENTIFIED
FLYING ELEPHANT

Story by ROBERT KRAUS

WINDMILL

BOOKS

Windmill Books, Inc. / Simon & Schuster, Inc.

New York